KT-504-782

SPACE SCHOOL
BLAST OFF!

Tom & Tony Bradman

Illustrated by Si Clark

A & C Black • London

SPACE SCHOOL

BLAST OFF!

04271560

For my co-author, from his Dad

First published 2011 by
A & C Black Publishers Ltd
36 Soho Square, London, W1D 3QY

www.acblack.com

Text copyright © 2011 Tony Bradman and Tom Bradman
Illustrations copyright © 2011 Si Clark

The rights of Tony Bradman, Tom Bradman and Si Clark to be
identified as the authors and illustrator of this work have been
asserted by them in accordance with the Copyrights,
Designs and Patents Act 1988.

ISBN 978-1-4081-2379-9

A CIP catalogue for this book is available from the British Library.

All rights reserved. No part of this publication may be
reproduced in any form or by any means – graphic, electronic
or mechanical, including photocopying, recording, taping or
information storage and retrieval systems – without
the prior permission in writing of the publishers.

This book is produced using paper that is made from wood
grown in managed, sustainable forests. It is natural, renewable and
recyclable. The logging and manufacturing processes conform
to the environmental regulations of the country of origin.

Printed and bound in Great Britain
by CPI Cox & Wyman, Reading, RG1 8EX.

CHAPTER ONE
A CLASS TRIP

'Now, are you *certain* you've got everything you need, Luke?' said Captain Riley. The two of them – a tall woman with short dark hair, and her son, the spitting image of her – were walking along the main access corridor of the United Earth spaceship *Buzz Aldrin*, their space boots clanging on the metal deck.

'Absolutely *positive*,' sighed Luke, shifting his bulging schoolbag from one shoulder to another. 'I'm only going on a class trip. Clarke said we'll be on the planet for a few hours, tops. You're making me take so much stuff, I could survive down there for *years*.'

'Sorry,' said Mum, slightly embarrassed. 'It's just that this is the first time you've been off the *Buzz Aldrin* since we left Earth, and I worry about you. Actually, I wish I were coming, too. I could do with some fresh air.'

Luke was looking forward to being out in the open himself. It was nearly a year since the remnants of humanity had fled a polluted Earth in a fleet of spaceships. They were searching for a new home, a planet they could colonise. But planets were few and very far between in the dark emptiness of space. Then at last they had found one that seemed possible, a medium-sized world with a breathable atmosphere orbiting a pair of suns.

For a while, excitement had buzzed through the *Buzz Aldrin*. The planet, however, had turned out to be a major disappointment, a barren ball of rock and sand without any plants or animals. The search would have to go on, but Luke's mum had put the *Buzz Aldrin* into a parking orbit so they could do some repairs, and she had agreed when Clarke, Luke's computer-generated teacher, had asked if he could organise a class trip.

'Well, you can stop worrying,' said Luke. 'Everything's going to be fine.'

They had reached the end of the corridor and Mum punched the entry code into the keypad next to the shuttle-bay doors.

'I'll do my best,' she said with a smile, and gave him a kiss as the doors hissed open. Luke rubbed his cheek with the sleeve of his parka and hurried inside, hoping none of his classmates had seen.

The shuttle bay was a large steel cavern with a high curved ceiling and a wide pair of doors in the hull wall. Inside was the shuttle itself. The small craft was designed to be used for short journeys between the *Buzz Aldrin* and planets or other spaceships. It was a chunky vessel the size of an old Earth-style minibus, with a cockpit at the front and a couple of stubby engine vents at the rear.

The rest of Luke's class were waiting with their parents. Mum went off to talk to the grown-ups, and Luke soon found Yasmin and Yuri, his best friends. He dropped his schoolbag on the deck, where it landed with a loud *CLUNK!*

'What have you got in there, Luke?' said Yasmin, raising an eyebrow. Her long brown hair was tied back in a ponytail and her coffee-coloured skin shone with health. All the kids had been told to wear a warm coat, and her parka was by far the most stylish. 'Anyone would think you were leaving home!'

'No such luck,' muttered Luke. 'How long before we get under way?'

'Clarke is just doing the pre-flight checks on the shuttle's systems,' said Yuri. He was small and skinny and red-haired, and his schoolbag was stuffed to the brim, too.

Luke guessed it contained Yuri's favourite laptop as well as loads of other electronic gadgets. 'Ah, here he comes now.'

Luke turned round and saw an elderly man with white hair and a droopy moustache emerging from the shuttle. Clarke was a hologram, and until recently he had been able to take on the appearance of any famous person in the ship's knowledge banks. But a major computer glitch – caused by Luke and his friends – had left him permanently stuck in the form of Albert Einstein.

'Good morning, Primary One and parents,' said Clarke in his quiet voice. 'It's lovely to see everyone. You children are in for a real treat today.'

'That sounds promising,' Luke whispered, exchanging grins with Yasmin and Yuri. But their smiles soon vanished.

'As you might know, my hobby is geology,' Clarke continued. 'So I've decided we're going to spend the day studying the planet's rocks. Right, everybody, on board now please.'

'Oh no,' groaned Yasmin, her shoulders slumping. 'How dull can you get?'

'Well, that's Clarke for you,' muttered Yuri. 'He's the Prince of Dullness.'

'Too right,' said Luke. 'Maybe I should ask Mum if we can have a new teacher. I'm beginning to think anyone would be better than him.' He picked up his schoolbag and trudged grimly towards the shuttle.

CHAPTER TWO
AN ALIEN WORLD

Getting the class into the shuttle turned out to be a tight squeeze, and there was lots of bad-tempered pushing and shoving as everyone found their seats.

'Ouch! Watch where you're putting your big feet, Luke!' said Yasmin.

'Just be grateful he didn't drop his bag on them,' said Yuri, laughing.

'Huh, you can talk,' Luke muttered, elbowing his way beyond his friends into a tiny space by a view-port. He tried to shove his bag beneath the seat, but it wouldn't fit, and he ended up with his legs draped over it uncomfortably.

'Settle down, everybody, please, and fasten your seatbelts,' said Clarke, from the pilot's seat. He touched a glowing square on the control panel and the shuttle door closed. Luke felt the engine throb into life.

'Hey, sir!' Yasmin said cheekily. 'Are you sure you can fly this thing?'

'You'd better hope so, Yasmin!' Clarke replied. A clanking sound resonated through the shuttle as the docking clamps were released. The bay's exterior doors opened and the shuttle rose from the deck. Clarke gave the engine more power, and the kids were pushed back in their seats.

Luke looked out of the view-port, and for a moment it seemed the *Buzz Aldrin* was shrinking, even though he knew that was just an illusion. Soon he could see the whole ship – the central axle over a kilometre in length, the huge engine pod at

one end, the colossal golf-ball-like guidance module containing the ship's bridge at the other. And halfway along the axle, spinning constantly to create their artificial gravity, was the giant wheel where everybody lived.

Beyond the ship lay the star-spotted blackness of space, but Luke's eyes were drawn to their destination. To begin with it was just a yellow and black object the size of a basketball, but gradually it grew until it filled the view-port. Clarke took them into the atmosphere at a steep angle, then quickly levelled out the shuttle.

Luke stared at the alien world below, the first he had ever seen this close. The suns were rising on the horizon and casting their light over the jagged yellow landscape. Endless rough cracks zigzagged across it, and enormous mountains cast shadows that seemed to stretch forever.

Luke frowned uneasily. The planet looked harsh and forbidding and rather scary. Suddenly, the shuttle lurched to one side and started to judder.

'Don't worry,' Clarke said over his shoulder. 'Just a little turbulence!'

'I'm going to throw up,' moaned Yuri, who had gone a nasty shade of green.

'If you're sick on me, it will be the last thing you ever do,' snapped Yasmin.

Fortunately, the journey didn't last long. Just seconds later Clarke brought the shuttle down to a smooth landing, and the juddering stopped.

'Phew, thank goodness for that!' muttered Yuri. 'Let me out of here.'

Clarke opened the door, and there was more pushing and shoving as the class disembarked. Luke still felt faintly uneasy, and was the last to step onto the surface of the planet. They had landed in what looked like a small valley, its bottom a flat expanse of coarse yellow sand, its sides dotted with large boulders. The air was crisp, which was good, but it was cold, too, and Luke was glad of his warm parka.

'Gather round,' said Clarke, grinning as if all his Christmases and birthdays had come at once. 'Isn't this just wonderful? I'd like you to take out your notepads and worksheets. I thought we could start by taking a look at the various rock strata in the area. Now, follow me!'

Most of the class did as they were told, but Yasmin held back her friends.

'There's no way I'm going to spend my time down here looking at a load of old rocks,' she said. 'Come on – let's go and do a bit of exploring of our own. Clarke will be so busy enjoying himself, he won't notice we've gone.'

'Sounds good to me,' said Yuri, who was his usual pale and freckly shade once more. 'What about you, Luke?'

'I don't know,' said Luke. 'I mean, what if we run into something dangerous? We've no idea what might be waiting out there...'

'Come on, don't be such a wimp,' said Yasmin. 'Your mum wouldn't have let Clarke bring us down here if the scans had detected anything *dangerous*.'

Luke shrugged. 'OK, Yasmin,' he said. 'You lead the way.' But for some reason he couldn't help crossing his fingers behind his back.

CHAPTER THREE
CAVE OF WONDERS

Yasmin looked round, then led her friends into a small gully at one end of the valley. It took them up to the valley rim, from where they could see a vast expanse of broken country, an endless landscape of yellow sand and rocks. Above them, the cloudless sky was a sickly orange with purple streaks.

'Well, it's not paradise, is it?' snorted Yasmin. 'You'd have to be a boring old hologram teacher whose hobby is studying rocks to love it.'

'What's that over there?' said Yuri, pointing. 'It looks like the mouth of a cave.'

'Might as well check it out,' said Yasmin.

'You never know, it might be the entrance to an underground alien theme park with rides and other cool stuff!'

'Yeah, right,' said Luke.

'Just kidding,' said Yasmin. 'OK, last one there has to carry Luke's bag!' She gave Yuri a high-five, then the two of them dashed down the outer slope of the valley, their boots kicking up a cloud of yellow dust.

Luke sighed and trudged after them. His bag seemed heavier than ever, and he began to think he should have left it behind in the shuttle. By the time he caught up with the others, he felt hot inside his parka, despite the chilly air.

'Hey, Luke, come and look at this!' Yuri called over to his friend. 'It's *awesome...*'

At once, Luke's mood lifted. Yuri was right. Inside the opening was a huge cavern, its far wall lost in shadow.

'I'd like to go in,' murmured Yasmin. 'But it's very dark.'

'No problem,' Luke said triumphantly. 'I've got a torch in my bag.'

He delved inside and got out the torch. It was a heavy-duty one, the kind used by repair crews on the *Buzz Aldrin*. Luke switched it on and the powerful beam shone out, slicing through the darkness as he moved it over the walls.

'You know, I don't think this is a natural cave,' said Yuri, suddenly serious. 'I mean, look at the floor and walls – they're almost totally smooth.'

'You're right,' said Luke. 'And are those doors over there?'

They walked further into the cavern and stood in front of a semi-circular opening five metres high. Several similar openings flanked it on either side, all of them sealed by slabs of dark metal covered in strange markings.

'Umm, nice decoration,' said Yasmin, peering closely at a swirl of flowing lines. 'I used to have a dress a bit like that. And what's this, a handprint?'

'It might be,' said Yuri, moving forward to look. 'Although it has only three fingers. It's cut into the door... Hey, maybe it's an opening mechanism of some kind!'

Yuri reached out, but Luke grabbed his arm. 'Don't touch it!' he warned. 'Maybe we should just go back and tell Clarke.'

'What, and get in trouble for sneaking off?' said Yasmin. 'I don't think so.'

'Hang on a second,' said Yuri. He had pulled a small gadget from his bag and was pointing it at the door. 'I'm picking up some kind of energy reading.'

'Which means there's something in there!' said Yasmin, her eyes shining. 'Well, Luke?'

'Oh, go on then,' said Luke with a shrug.

Yasmin grinned and then whacked her palm down hard on the dark metal. Nothing happened at first, but then the handprint began to give off a weird alien glow, a yellow light that shone right through Yasmin's hand. A grinding noise followed and the slab split down the middle, each half sliding into the walls on either side. Luke shone his torch into a dark passage.

'After you, Luke,' said Yasmin. 'You're the one in charge of the torch.'

'Oh, so suddenly *I'm* the leader, am I?' Luke muttered. But he was curious now, despite his doubts, and he headed into the passage. It was long and narrow, with several twists and turns.

After a while, they walked out onto a wide balcony overlooking a massive chamber. In the centre was a huge golden sphere crackling with energy. It was throbbing, too, pushing pulses of purple light through transparent tubes that snaked out of it and covered the chamber's floor and walls. Just like a giant heart pumping blood around the veins of a body, Luke thought. He shivered at the strangeness of the sight.

'*Not* a theme park, then,' Yasmin said. 'Pretty cool, though! What do you –'

Suddenly, a glowing figure seemed to appear out of the air in front of the sphere. A huge, purple, android-like creature with two arms and two legs, a smooth, featureless body, a round face with a black line where its eyes should have been, and a shorter line for a mouth. The kids stared at it, wide-eyed.

'I told you we shouldn't have come in here,' Luke murmured.

CHAPTER FOUR
INVASION THREAT

'Relax, Luke, you worry too much,' said Yuri, a big grin on his face. He pulled another gadget out of his bag and pointed it at the android. 'This is absolutely incredible. A real alien being. No, wait a minute, it's a hologram!'

'Like Clarke?' said Luke, rather surprised, although it made sense. 'I suppose that would explain how it just appeared out of thin air.'

'So you don't think we're in any danger from it, then?' said Yasmin.

'No idea,' said Yuri. 'I can tell you one thing, though – it's scanning us.'

Luke looked more closely at the hologram and saw purple light pulsing along the line at the top of its face. The golden sphere was crackling more, too. Then the pulsing stopped, but before they could say anything, the hologram spoke.

'*ORGANIC LIFE FORMS HAVE BEEN DETECTED!*' it said, its voice booming out and echoing round the chamber. '*IDENTIFY YOURSELVES!*'

Yasmin opened her mouth to speak, but Luke held up his hand. 'I think you should let me do the talking, Yasmin,' he said. 'You can be a bit tactless.'

'Is that so? Well, be my guest,' said Yasmin, giving him a dirty look.

Luke took no notice, and turned to address the hologram. 'My name is Luke Riley, and these are my friends Yuri and Yasmin,' he said. 'Who are you?'

'*I AM PLANETARY DEFENCE UNIT ALPHA*,' the hologram boomed.

'Fascinating,' murmured Yuri. 'Ask who created it in the first place.'

'I was just about to!' Luke hissed. 'Who created you in the –'

'*THE MAKERS*,' Alpha boomed. '*THEY WERE ORGANIC AND HAD TO BE DESTROYED LONG AGO. ALPHA HAS BEEN ALONE... UNTIL TODAY.*'

Luke glanced at Yuri and Yasmin, and raised his eyebrows. 'I hope you don't mind me asking,' he said. 'But why did these... *Makers* have to be destroyed?'

'*ALPHA WILL SHOW YOU*,' boomed the hologram. Suddenly pictures began to scroll across the golden sphere, images of a great civilisation – amazing cities and machines built by a race of tall, thin aliens with three-fingered hands. '*THE MAKERS CREATED ALPHA TO DEFEND THE PLANET FROM INVASION*,' Alpha boomed. '*BUT THEN THEY DECIDED TO SWITCH ALPHA OFF...*'

'They probably got fed up with the sound of its voice,' muttered Yasmin. 'I mean, I bet it's even more boring than old Clarke when it really gets going.'

'*SO ALPHA HAD TO DESTROY THEM AND CLEANSE THE SURFACE OF THE*

PLANET,' boomed the hologram, and paused. 'YOU ARE ORGANIC,' it said at last. 'ALL ORGANIC LIFE FORMS ARE A THREAT TO ALPHA.'

The line at the top of Alpha's head began pulsing with purple light again, but more intensely this time. The pulsing in the tubes seemed to have speeded up as well, and the sphere crackled so strongly that bolts leapt from it to Alpha.

'Now hang on a second,' said Luke. 'You shouldn't judge us by these Makers of yours. We're just some human beings looking for a new home.'

'NEW HOME?' boomed Alpha even more loudly. 'ALERT! INVASION THREAT CONFIRMED. ORGANIC LIFE FORMS MUST BE DESTROYED!'

The purple pulsing in the tubes went crazy, and the golden sphere crackled like a machine in a mad scientist's laboratory. Alpha was humming ominously.

'Great job, Luke!' muttered Yasmin.

Alpha lifted its arms and fired two bolts of purple energy from its hands. The kids ducked just in time, and the bolts *ZAPPED!* into the roof of the passage above them, blowing a big hole in it.

Then Alpha slowly floated up until it was hovering above the balcony, its whole body now pulsing with purple fire.

'Guys, I think we should probably –' said Luke, his voice trailing away, eyes locked on the vision before him.

Yuri was equally transfixed, his mouth open.

'I think the word you're looking for,' Yasmin whispered, 'is *RUN!*' She yelled the last word, and the sound of her voice echoing in the chamber brought Luke and Yuri to their senses.

They turned and raced back down the passage. Purple bolts slammed into the walls around them and the floor near their heels, so Luke knew they were being followed. He also realised his bag was slowing him down. He spun round, slipping it off his shoulder as he turned, and threw it straight at Alpha. But it passed right through the hologram's body and merely went skidding along the floor, back towards the balcony.

Another bolt hit the wall close to Luke, showering him with bits of rock and dust. He sprinted after his friends, and seconds later they emerged from the cavern.

'Keep moving,' panted Yuri. 'We have to get back to the shuttle!'

Luke couldn't have agreed more. But they all knew Alpha wasn't far behind.

CHAPTER FIVE
BADLY BEHAVED

They scrambled back up the slope of the valley in a cloud of yellow dust and dashed through the same gully, emerging by the shuttle at last. Clarke was coming round the front of the small craft and looked relieved to see them.

'Ah, there you are!' he said as they ran up to him and stopped, their faces red, their chests heaving. 'Where have you been? I thought for a while you might have sneaked off, but I know you are far too sensible to do anything quite so silly. We are on an alien planet, after all, and –'

'Big cavern ... purple bolts ... chased by

a hologram!' Luke panted, desperately trying to catch his breath so he could speak properly. He gestured vaguely at Yuri and Yasmin, hoping they would be able to explain, but they were even more breathless than him. 'Coming here ... any minute,' he panted. 'Shuttle ... quick ... please!'

'What in *space* are you talking about, Luke?' said Clarke, frowning. 'Just slow down and try to tell me what you've seen. You're not hurt, are you?'

Luke shook his head and took in great gulps of air. But before he could start speaking again, he heard a familiar humming noise. Then there was a loud *ZAP!*, followed by several more *ZAP!*s and screams of panic.

Clarke's frown deepened and he strode off, back round the shuttle. Luke, Yasmin and Yuri hurried after him, but they skidded to a halt when they saw what was happening. Three balls of purple energy now hovered over the valley, firing bolts downwards, almost as if they were herding their classmates into a huddle. None of the children had been hurt, but they were clearly terrified.

'This is terrible!' said Clarke. 'It must be some kind of strange atmospheric phenomenon. Over here, everyone! Take shelter in the shuttle!'

'It's got nothing to do with the atmosphere, sir,' said Luke, his breath under control at last. 'I'll bet it's Alpha who's controlling those ball things.'

'Alpha?' said Clarke, confused. '*Now* what are you talking about, Luke?'

'Well, it's kind of difficult to explain,' said Luke.

Suddenly, Yuri tugged his sleeve. Luke turned to look at his friend, but all Yuri did was point into the sky.

Alpha was descending into the valley, like a superhero coming in to land after a flight through the heavens. The three balls of purple energy stopped firing their bolts, although they stayed in position above the rest of the class.

'I wish *I* could do that,' Yasmin murmured with admiration. 'And the firing-energy-bolts-thing. I still don't like it much, though.'

'Would somebody *please* tell me what's going on?' said Clarke.

It was too late, however. Before they could say another word, Alpha arrived in front of them, the line at the top of its head pulsing away. Luke closed his eyes, expecting to be burned to a crisp at any second, but there was no purple flash. So he opened his eyes... and realised Alpha was scanning Clarke.

'*YOU ARE LIKE ALPHA!*' boomed the alien, its voice just as loud in the open air. '*BEWARE! THESE ORGANIC LIFE FORMS ARE DANGEROUS!*'

'Organic life forms?' said Clarke. 'Oh, you mean the *children*. They can be badly behaved sometimes, but I don't think you could call them dangerous.' He paused for a moment, then turned to look sternly at the class. 'Although that really depends on what they get up to, I suppose. Does anyone have anything to tell me?'

'Well,' Luke stammered. 'The truth is that we *did* sneak off, sir. And we found this... this *being* in an amazing cavern near here...'

'You should see the place, sir!' Yuri said eagerly. 'It's incredible! Alpha was created by a civilisation that was much more advanced than ours.'

'In that case, I'm certain we can make friends with him, or it, or whatever it is,' murmured Clarke.

'I wouldn't be so sure,' said Yasmin. 'It's got a very short temper.'

'Now, Yasmin,' said Clarke. 'That's not a very nice thing to say.'

'*SILENCE!*' boomed Alpha, purple energy crackling furiously all over it. Clarke winced. '*ARE THE ORGANIC LIFE FORMS IMPORTANT TO YOU?*'

'Of *course* they are,' said Clarke. 'So I'm afraid I can't let you destroy them. But let me know if there's anything else I can do for you.'

'*YOU ARE LIKE ALPHA*,' boomed Alpha once more. '*YOU MUST STAY WITH ALPHA FOREVER. THEN ALPHA WILL NO LONGER BE ALONE.*'

'Oh, I couldn't possibly do that,' said Clarke, taken aback.

Alpha paused for a moment, almost as if it were thinking. '*ALPHA WILL LET THE ORGANIC LIFE FORMS LEAVE THE PLANET IF YOU AGREE TO STAY*,' it said at last. '*IF YOU DO NOT, ALPHA WILL DESTROY THEM.*'

CHAPTER SIX
NET OF ENERGY

Now it was Luke's turn to frown. He hadn't expected Alpha to bargain with Clarke. Yasmin and Yuri looked pretty shocked, too.

'Huh, crafty as well as nasty,' Yasmin muttered. 'That is *so* not a winning combo. And I wouldn't be cocn deau in that particular shade of purple, either.'

'I don't think you'll be purple if it zaps you, Yasmin,' Yuri hissed. 'More a kind of ash-grey with a few charred bits and lots of white smoke.'

'Could it really – ?' Clarke muttered nervously from the side of his mouth.

'Destroy the class?' whispered Luke. 'Oh yes, definitely, no doubt about it.'

Yuri and Yasmin were nodding vigorously, but then they all ducked, even Clarke. Alpha had heard what Luke had said, and raised a hand to demonstrate his power by firing a bolt of purple energy at a large rock just behind them. The rock was blown to pieces, and at the same time the three balls of energy hovering over the rest of the class started to crackle ominously.

'OK, stop shooting!' yelled Clarke, holding up his hands. 'We surrender!'

'*SO YOU AGREE TO STAY FOREVER?*' boomed Alpha, lowering his hand.

'Yes, if it's the only way to stop you hurting the children,' said Clarke.

'But... but you can't do that, sir!' spluttered Luke.

'Oh, don't worry, Luke,' said Clarke, smiling at him. 'I can set the auto-pilot on the shuttle. It will take everybody straight back to the *Buzz Aldrin* –'

'That's not what I meant,' said Luke. 'You live on the *Buzz Aldrin* with us. You're our teacher. You can't stay here forever with some strange alien being!'

'Luke's right,' agreed Yasmin. 'Who knows what that... that *thing* will do to you once we're gone?'

'On the other hand, it might be OK,' Yuri said cheerfully. 'You might learn a lot from Alpha. After all, it *is* the product of an advanced civilisation.' Yasmin glared at him. 'Or maybe not,' Yuri added hurriedly.

'*THERE HAS BEEN FAR TOO MUCH TALKING!*' boomed Alpha. '*IT IS TIME FOR ALL THE ORGANIC LIFE FORMS TO LEAVE THE PLANET!*'

'You'd better go before he starts shooting again,' said Clarke, scowling at Alpha. 'Tell your mother what's happened, Luke,' he whispered. 'She'll need to make sure the *Buzz Aldrin* is safe from whatever else Alpha might do. Right, Primary One, everybody into the shuttle now, please.'

Luke could tell there was no arguing with his teacher. The class hurried onto the shuttle, most of the kids more than happy to escape from the crackling purple balls of energy that followed them. Luke, Yasmin and Yuri were the last to go on board.

'Quick, sir!' Luke hissed. 'Let's just shut

the door and make a break for it!'

'I don't think that would work, Luke,' said Clarke, nodding at Alpha, who was right by the door, peering into the shuttle. 'He'd probably shoot us down.'

'*YOUR ASSESSMENT OF THE SITUATION IS ACCURATE,*' said Alpha.

So Luke took his seat with Yasmin and Yuri while Clarke did the pre-flight system checks and set the auto-pilot. At last everything was ready for take-off.

'OK, strap yourselves in,' said Clarke, looking sad. 'Take care of yourselves. Perhaps one day we'll –'

'*YOU WILL COME WITH ALPHA NOW!*' boomed the hologram, firing a purple pulse at Clarke. But this one was different. It appeared to be made up of thin lines that expanded on contact, snaring their teacher in a net of energy. Clarke was yanked out of the shuttle and Alpha flew off, the three balls following.

Most of the children in the class were crying. Luke, Yasmin and Yuri, however, sat in their seats looking thoughtful. Luke could feel the shuttle's engine throbbing, and see the countdown to take-off ticking away on the cockpit control panel. The shuttle door began to close slowly as well.

'You know, he wasn't *really* all that boring, was he?' Yuri murmured.

'You're right,' said Yasmin. 'In fact, sometimes he could be a lot of fun.'

'And he didn't stop to think when it came to sacrificing himself for us, did he?' said Luke. 'Even though it was because of us that this happened.'

They sat quietly for a moment, the engine noise growing stronger, the door almost closed now. Then Yasmin looked at her friends, her eyes narrowed.

'We can't just sit here and do nothing,' she said. 'Going back to the *Buzz Aldrin* for help will take too long. I vote that we save our teacher ... ourselves.'

'I'm glad you said that,' Luke answered, grinning. 'I was thinking the same thing.'

'Come on, then,' said Yuri. 'Let's get out of here while we still can.'

The three of them jumped to their feet and made a dash for the door.

CHAPTER SEVEN
BUNDLE OF WIRES

Luke and his friends watched the shuttle take off in a cloud of yellow dust, its speed turning it into a tiny dot that disappeared in the orange and purple sky. The three of them then ran back to the cavern as fast as they could, keeping an eye out for any of Alpha's lethal flying energy balls.

Yasmin was about to go through the same doorway as before when Luke grabbed her by the arm.

'Hold on a second,' he said. 'I bet Alpha's got Clarke in the room with the sphere. If he sees us coming, we're in big trouble. We have to *sneak* in, creep up behind them.

Let's try one of these other doors.'

'All right then, clever-clogs,' said Yasmin.
'Any idea which one?'

Luke shrugged. 'Ip dip, sky blue...' he said,
pointing at the doors one by one. 'Who's it,
not *YOU!*' He quickly moved forward and
slammed his hand down on the opening
mechanism of the winning door. 'Come on,
guys!' he said.

This new corridor looked much the
same as the last one, although it had more
twists and turns. There were also a lot of
other corridors branching off it. Every time
they came to a junction, Luke simply made
a guess and didn't stop. They passed room
after room full of alien computers and
strange gadgets. Soon, Luke didn't have
a clue where they were, or how to get to
the room with the sphere.

'Wait!' yelled Yasmin from behind him.

'We're lost – this place is a maze.'

'Lost?' squeaked Yuri. 'Oh, great, maybe we'll be trapped in here forever.'

'Don't blame me,' said Luke. 'It's not exactly like I've got a map, is it?'

'A map...' Yuri had a faraway look in his eyes, and suddenly snapped his fingers. 'That's it!' He ran back a little way and darted into a small room.

Yasmin and Luke looked at each other, then followed him. When they got to the door, Luke couldn't believe his eyes. Yuri had yanked a huge bundle of wires out from under some weird alien device. Sparks were flying everywhere, but Yuri had plugged one of the wires into his laptop and didn't seem to notice.

'What are you *doing*, Yuri?' said Luke. 'We don't have time for this!'

'Relax, I'm being a genius, that's all,' Yuri

said, grinning. 'If I can just find the cipher...'
he muttered, tapping at the laptop. After
a while, a series of alien symbols began to
appear on the screen, only to be replaced
by lines and shapes that reminded Luke of
something.

'That's it, I'm in!' Yuri said, grinning even
more. 'I have complete logarithmic access
to Alpha's data storage.'

'Way too much geek-speak, Yuri,' said
Yasmin. 'Translation, please!'

'Ta da! We have a map!' Yuri said
triumphantly. He pointed at the screen of
the laptop. 'This is where we are, and...'
he tapped at his keyboard again and the
picture changed. 'This must be the room
with the sphere. Come on – it's not far!'

They soon got there. Reaching the end of a corridor, they realised they were looking out from one side of the original balcony. Luke noticed his bag still lying where it had landed, up against the railing. But more importantly, they had found Clarke. Their teacher was standing beneath the huge sphere, being talked at by Alpha. Luke got the impression that it was a very boring lecture.

'*AND AFTER I SOLVED THE LAST PROBABILITY DYSFUNCTION EQUATION, MY INTELLECTUAL SUPERIORITY WAS UNDENIABLE...*'

'Fascinating,' said Clarke, his eyes glazed.

'*IT WAS DURING A LECTURE I GAVE ON THE SUBJECT THAT THE MAKERS ATTEMPTED TO DISCONNECT MY POWER SOURCE...*'

'Told you,' hissed Yasmin, nudging Luke and grinning. 'Bored witless.'

'*AND SO I WAS FORCED TO ELIMINATE THEM.*' Amazingly, even with no features on its face, Alpha still managed to look smug.

'Bored *to death*...' whispered Luke. A shiver travelled down his spine.

'*AND NOW I WILL DEMONSTRATE THE SUPERIORITY OF ALPHA AGAIN!*' Alpha raised an arm, and a stream of purple energy crackled from it. Suddenly, an image began to take shape in the middle of the chamber – a perfect, three-dimensional picture of the *Buzz Aldrin*. *'I HAVE DETECTED THE VESSEL IN ORBIT,'* boomed Alpha. *'IT WILL BE DESTROYED!'*

'But you promised you'd let them go!' said Clarke, horrified. 'Why do you want to hurt them? They've done nothing to you.'

'YOUR IRRATIONAL ATTACHMENT TO THE ORGANIC LIFE FORMS HAS CORRUPTED YOUR PROGRAMMING,' Alpha was saying. *'YOU ARE DEFECTIVE. BUT ALPHA WILL REMOVE THE DEFECT. ALL ORGANIC LIFE FORMS MUST BE ELIMINATED. ELIMINATED! ELIMINATED!'*

Luke heard Yasmin draw in her breath sharply. 'I was right!' she muttered. 'I never trusted that thing from the moment I laid eyes on it.'

CHAPTER EIGHT
CRITICAL DAMAGE

'Oh no,' Luke groaned softly. 'This can't be happening...'

An ominous circle of purple light had appeared around the image of the *Buzz Aldrin*, and the pulsing in the tubes began to grow in intensity. For a brief instant, Luke froze, unable to speak. Panic ran through his veins like the energy throbbing in the chamber. Then he took a deep breath, and pulled himself together.

'OK, listen up, guys,' he whispered. In the chamber below, he could see Clarke pleading with Alpha, but the alien was ignoring him. 'I am not about to let the most boring hologram in the universe destroy everyone on board the *Buzz Aldrin*, including my mum. We *have* to stop it. Any suggestions?'

Yasmin shook her head, her eyes wide. But Yuri smiled.

'Just give me a minute,' he said. He whipped out his laptop and tapped away furiously, all kinds of diagrams and figures whizzing across the screen. 'The sphere,' he murmured after a while. 'I'm pretty sure it's Alpha's power source. It's channelling energy from somewhere. Now, if we could disable it...'

'What, you mean switch it off?' asked Yasmin. 'How? Alpha's right beside it!'

'I don't know yet,' Yuri snapped. 'I'm still trying to find out!'

'Well, get a move on,' hissed Yasmin. 'This is serious!'

'Like I don't know that,' muttered Yuri, eyes fixed on the screen, his fingers still tapping away. 'Hey, now that *is* interesting...'

'For heaven's sake, Yuri,' snarled Yasmin. 'Don't have a geek attack now!'

The two of them kept arguing, and Luke stopped listening. The throbbing in the chamber was reaching a climax, and the golden sphere was crackling with huge bursts of purple energy. It looked as if there was nothing they could do.

Then Luke's eyes fell on his bag, the big, heavy bag his mum had packed with everything she could think of to keep him safe. Good old Mum, he thought, glancing up. Maybe the sphere was more fragile than it looked?

Luke smiled, grabbed the strap of his bag, and quickly rose to his feet. Then he started swinging the bag round his head like someone throwing the hammer at an athletics event. Soon he was spinning round and round, faster and faster.

'*INTRUDER! INTRUDER!*' boomed Alpha. But it was too late. Before Alpha could do anything, Luke let go of the strap. The bag flew across the chamber and hit the sphere, smashing through its outer surface. The throbbing and energy pulses in the chamber all paused for a second ... and then the sphere exploded with a huge *BANG!*, chunks of metal and golden glass flying everywhere.

Luke, Yasmin and Yuri dived for cover, and for a while all Luke could hear was a fierce crackling. Eventually, the noise died down and the three of them peeked over the railing. Alpha was still there, although now it was motionless and silent. Clarke was all right, though he did look shocked.

'What are you doing here?' he said. 'I thought I told you to –'

Suddenly, a whining noise came from Alpha, like a computer re-booting itself. Purple light began to pulse in the line at the top of its head once more.

'*WARNING!*' Alpha boomed. '*CRITICAL DAMAGE SUSTAINED TO ENTIRE SYSTEM! INITIATING SELF-DESTRUCT PROTOCOL! PLANET CORE DETONATION IN FIVE MINUTES AND COUNTING! WARNING...*'

'I don't like the sound of that,' said Luke. 'Is it as bad as I think, Yuri?'

'It's our worst nightmare,' said Yuri, tapping at his laptop. 'The sphere drew its power from the planet's core and Alpha's still linked to it.'

'Nice one, Luke,' sighed Yasmin. 'Looks like it's game over.'

'I don't know about that,' said Yuri. 'I tried to tell you a while back, but you wouldn't listen. I think I've found us a ride out of here. There's a shuttle bay –'

'Why didn't you say so sooner?' said Luke. 'Come on, let's get going!'

They found another door into the chamber and gathered up Clarke, then they raced along the corridors towards the shuttle bay, following Yuri's directions. Lines of purple energy crackled over the ceilings, and Luke could feel the ground rumbling through the soles of his space boots.

Eventually, Yasmin skidded to a halt. Luke and Yuri almost crashed into her.

'Hey, watch out!' said Luke.

But Yasmin took no notice of him. She was staring straight ahead, her eyes like saucers. 'Check... it... out!' she said. 'Is that cool, or what?'

Sitting in the centre of the cavern was the sleekest spaceship Luke had ever seen. If the *Buzz Aldrin*'c shuttle was like a minibus, then this was like an incredible sports car or speedboat.

Luckily, the hatch was open and they all piled inside. The interior looked quite alien, of course, but there were four seats, a view-screen and a control panel.

'I've just thought of a problem,' said Yasmin. 'Does anyone know –'

'How to fly this thing?' said Clarke, smiling. 'Leave it to me.'

Clarke sat in the pilot's seat and the children strapped themselves in.

'I don't want to worry anyone,' said Yuri. 'But we've only got ten seconds...'

'Just firing up the engine,' said Clarke. He touched a glowing square on the control panel and the shuttle rose.

Luke glanced through the view-screen and saw that the whole ceiling of the chamber was opening.

'*BLAST OFF!*'

Then he was pressed back into his seat as

shuttle shot upwards and out. Luke caught a glimpse of jagged cracks in yellow sand and dark mountains, and then they were in space, accelerating away from the planet as fast as they could go.

Suddenly they heard a huge *BOOM!*, and chunks of the planet flew past them, crackling with purple energy. The spaceship juddered, then steadied.

'Here we go again,' moaned Yuri, his face green. 'I feel really sick...'

'Don't worry, Yuri,' said Clarke, 'we'll soon be back on the *Buzz Aldrin*. What an awful creature Alpha was! Please tell me I'm never that boring.'

'Oh no, sir, not at all,' said Luke. 'You're always very interesting!'

Yasmin couldn't look at him, and they both sat there shaking with silent laughter. But Luke knew they were pleased to have their old teacher back. Life on the *Buzz Aldrin* just wouldn't have been the same without him.